THE OUTFIT #4

THE GHOSTS OF GIVENHAM

Robert Swindells

ISBN 978-1-78270-056-2

Illustrations by Leo Hartas

First published by Scholastic Ltd 1993
This edition published by Award Publications Limited 2014

Published by Award Publications Limited,
The Old Riding School, The Welbeck Estate,
Worksop, Nottinghamshire, S80 3LR

www.awardpublications.co.uk

14 1

Printed in the United Kingdom

CONTENTS

THE GHOSTS OF
GIVENHAM KEEP

CHAPTER 1

READY TO GO

"What about the haunted house, then?"

"Huh?" Mickey shielded his eyes from the morning sun and scowled at the two Denton girls. "What're you on about?"

"The haunted house," repeated Jillo. "It's sold. Somebody's moved in."

"Never." Mickey was sitting on the caravan step, munching a bacon sandwich. The caravan stood in a clearing on the edge of Weeping Wood. It belonged to Mickey's dad, who was away as usual. Inside, Mickey's dog Raider was eating *his* breakfast at the table. Raider was a lurcher but he thought he was human.

"It's true," confirmed Titch. "Dad told Mum at breakfast. Apparently it's a bit of a mystery because nobody knows who he is."

"Well," Mickey tossed the last bit of his

sandwich into the bushes, stood up and brushed crumbs from his tattered jeans. "If it's a mystery, it's up to The Outfit to solve it. That's what we're good at, isn't it?"

"Sure is," grinned Jillo, "and we've six whole weeks to do it in. Where's Shaz?"

Mickey shrugged. "On his way probably, unless he's gone straight to HQ." HQ was the hut Farmer Denton had given them. It stood in a corner of one of his fields.

Titch shook her head. "We came past just now. He's not there."

"Yip!" Raider came to the door and stood gazing into the trees, growling softly. Mickey ruffled the coarse hair on the dog's neck. "Easy, Raider." He grinned at the girls. "This'll be him now."

It was. He came out of the trees and joined them round the step.

"Hi, everybody. Anything happening?"

"Funny you should say that, Shaz," chirped Titch. "Second day of the hols and we've found ourselves a mystery."

"You're kidding, right?"

"We are *not*," said Jillo. "Listen."

Briefly, she told him what her father had said

about the spooky derelict mansion, beyond the wood, they called the haunted house. When she'd finished, Shaz pulled a face. "They must be mad, whoever they are. Who'd want to live in a great echoing dump like that?"

Mickey thumped his arm. "That's the mystery, Shaz old son. I vote we get on to it straight away."

"I vote we do something first," said Titch.

"We know," chorused the others. "The oath." They joined hands in a circle with Raider in the middle and chanted:

"Faithful, fearless, full of fun,
Winter, summer, rain or sun,
One for five and five for one –
THE OUTFIT!"

On the last word they leapt high in the air and Raider barked. The Outfit was ready to go.

CHAPTER 2

WE'LL BE BACK

Sunlight filtered through the foliage of Weeping Wood and lay like a shower of gold doubloons across its spongy floor. Raider coursed to and fro in front of the children with his nose down, sniffing for rabbits. He found none, but succeeded now and then in startling birds, which flapped off screeching into the dim green distance.

Presently the trees thinned out and a high wall of mossy brick could be glimpsed between them. Mickey called the dog to heel and brought the party to a halt.

"Okay," he murmured, "this is it. I suggest we turn right, follow the wall to the corner and creep along to the gateway. If there's nothing to be seen from there and nobody's about, we'll go up the driveway. Keep it quiet from now on."

As they neared the wall, they noticed that metal posts had been fixed at intervals along its top to support three strands of barbed wire. The posts were angled outwards so that would-be intruders couldn't drape coats or sacks over the wire to neutralize the barbs. "Somebody doesn't want visitors," hissed Jillo. "I wonder if it's electrified as well?"

They reached the corner from which the great gateposts were visible. Stone griffins crouched on top of the posts, their heads wreathed in the foliage of the ancient trees which grew inside the grounds and overhung the wall. A poor road, perpetually in the shadow of the trees and scarred with cracks and potholes, ran parallel to the wall. The children advanced cautiously, creeping along the strip of grass and rank weeds that separated the wall from the road. Few vehicles ever came this way but they kept their ears open, ready to duck into the weeds at the sound of a motor.

No motor came, but a shock awaited them when they reached the gateway, because whoever had topped the wall with wire had also hung a pair of ugly steel gates on the posts.

They were about ten feet high, they didn't match the gateposts and they were closed.

"Oh heck!" moaned Mickey. "How are we supposed to spy on whoever lives here when we can't even see in?"

"We're obviously *not* supposed to spy," whispered Shaz.

"Hey," cried Titch, "look what it says on the gates. GIVENHAM KEEP. What the heck does *that* mean?"

"It's a name," said Jillo. "They've decided to call the house Givenham Keep. Think it sounds posh I suppose. If it was mine I'd call it Givenham Nightmares."

Everybody laughed. They were supposed to keep the noise down but there was nobody about, and anyway, you've got to have a bit of fun some time. Nobody noticed Raider leave Mickey's side and go sniffing along the foot of the gates till there came a volley of barks and growls and something heavy hurled itself at the gates from the inside, making them rattle.

"Raider!" roared Mickey. "Come here, you barmy mutt." He turned to the others. "Guard dogs. Let's get out of here before the row brings someone running."

They turned and pelted back along the strip. Beyond the wall the dogs kept pace with them, barking and growling till they reached the corner and plunged thankfully into Weeping Wood, running on till the wall was far behind. "Thank goodness dogs can't climb," gasped Titch when they finally stopped. "It must be a heck of a secret they're hiding at Givenham Keep."

Mickey, hugging a tree to keep from falling over, nodded. "Must be, Titch, but they can't hide it from us, whatever it is, 'cause we're The Outfit." He took a deep breath and shouted in the direction of the haunted house. "WE'RE THE OUTFIT, AND WE'LL BE BACK!" He looked at his dog. "Won't we, boy?"

"Yip!" said Raider.

CHAPTER 3

NOUGHTS AND CROSSES

"So what's our next move?" asked Titch when, half and hour later, the friends were seated round the table at Outfit HQ.

"Hard to say," grunted Mickey, "considering we can't even look over the wall."

"I think there's only one thing we can do," said Jillo.

Shaz looked at her. "Go on."

"Well, they can put up wire and steel gates and have guard dogs and all that, but they can't produce their own food and clothes and medicine in there, so they have to come out some time, if only to go shopping. I suggest we make a den in the weeds by the gate, and take turns watching them come and go. We could learn quite a lot that way."

"Such as what?" asked Mickey.

"Such as how many people go in and out, what they look like, whether visitors call – all sorts of stuff. We'd need to make notes."

"Hmm. Sounds a bit boring."

"Detective work *is* boring," retorted Jillo.

"We'd have to be careful, too," said Shaz. "I wouldn't fancy being spotted and having those dogs set on me."

"And talking of dogs," put in Mickey, "we'd have to leave Raider at home. He's not going to sit in a clump of thistles all day when there's Rottweilers to wind up."

"Ruff," confirmed Raider from his basket by the stove. Everybody laughed.

Jillo glanced round the table. "Anybody else got any bright ideas?"

Titch shook her head. "Not me."

"Me neither," said Shaz.

"Okay," said Mickey. "Your plan's adopted, Jillo. Why don't we all go together this time, and split into shifts later?"

This was agreed, and the meeting ended. It was lunchtime. The children arranged to meet at the caravan at half past two. "Bring pencils and something to write on," said Jillo, "then if it gets too boring at least we can play noughts and crosses."

CHAPTER 4

A MOVING SHADOW

"Well, *that* was a big waste of time," grumbled Titch. It was seven o'clock. The friends were trudging home through Weeping Wood after watching the gates of Givenham Keep for three and a half hours. "Nothing in, nothing out, and we've missed tea."

"We'd some good games of noughts and crosses though," grinned Shaz.

"Great," sneered Titch. "Why don't we disband The Outfit and start an outdoor noughts and crosses league instead?"

"Quit moaning, you little runt," growled Jillo. "You're getting on my nerves."

"Hey!" cried Mickey. "It's the first day, remember. It wouldn't be a decent mystery if we cracked it the first day. It'll be more interesting tomorrow, you'll see."

18

"That wouldn't be hard," muttered Titch. "I've had more excitement watching moss grow."

Shaz and the girls had to go home as soon as they reached the caravan, so Mickey fried burgers for Raider and himself and they ate them on the step as the sun sank beyond the trees. By the time he'd washed and stacked the tin plates it was dusk. "C'mon boy," he said. "Let's go scare some rabbits."

Mickey travelled in a great circle round the wood while Raider dashed in and out of thickets, yipping and snuffling and waving his tail. Raider was a lurcher and could have caught a rabbit if he'd wanted to, but he wasn't hungry. He just enjoyed the chase.

It was dark when Mickey completed his great circle and stepped into the clearing where the caravan stood. As he did so, Raider stopped and growled. Mickey stopped too. "What is it, boy?" he murmured. "Visitors?" Raider growled again, his muzzle pointing towards their home. "Okay." Mickey bent and picked up a heavy stick. "Easy, boy. Easy." He tiptoed forward, the dog at his heel. The caravan door stood open and he could just hear somebody clumping about inside. A sharp scratch was followed by the flare of a match which cast a moving shadow on the window blind. Mickey was ten paces away from the door when Raider yipped. The match was extinguished at once and a dark figure erupted from the caravan and pelted for the trees. The dog lunged after it.

"Raider!" Mickey called the animal to heel and entered the caravan, switching on the battery-powered light. The intruder had ransacked the food cupboard, scattering tins and sugar on the floor and slices of bread on the table. Otherwise, everything looked normal except the door lock, which was smashed. Mickey hefted his stick and looked at Raider. "Okay, boy," he growled. "Let's go get him."

CHAPTER 5

VICTOR

It never gets completely dark in July, but under the trees it was murky to say the least. Mickey held Raider in check till he was sure the dog wasn't following a rabbit, then said, "Okay. Boy – go get him." Raider bounded ahead with a yip and Mickey followed as best he could, his excellent night vision enabling him to avoid obstacles. He knew the intruder could be half a mile away by now, but nobody outruns a lurcher once it has the scent. In the event, their quarry had gone no further than a few hundred yards before seeking refuge in the crotch of an ancient oak, and Mickey found Raider standing at the foot of the tree, barking up at the foliage.

"Okay," he snapped, brandishing his stick. "Either you come down now or I leave my dog on guard and fetch the police." He couldn't see the fugitive but he was there all right. Raider was never wrong. There was a brief pause, then a voice said, "I didn't mean any harm. I was starving. I took some bread and cheese, that's all." It was a boy's voice.

"Come on down then," said Mickey. "I won't hurt you."

"What about your dog? I don't like dogs."

"He won't hurt you either, unless I tell him to, in which case he'll rip you to bits. Come down."

There was some rustling and scrabbling and a boy dropped out of the tree in a shower of twigs and leaves. He was a bit taller than Mickey, but very thin. He wore a sloppy jumper with holes and a pair of ragged blue jeans. He had battered trainers on his feet and a half-eaten hunk of cheese in his right fist. He stood looking from Raider to Mickey and back again. "I didn't expect a kid."

Mickey shook his head. "Neither did I. Where you from?"

"Nowhere."

Mickey smiled. "Everybody's from somewhere. Why are you starving?"

" 'Cause I'm on the run."

"Where from – prison?"

"No."

"Detention Centre?"

"No. I'm no criminal."

"Where, then? Have you been battered or something?"

"Something like that."

"So the cops aren't after you?"

"Are they heck, no."

"But somebody is?"

The boy nodded. "Somebody is."

"Okay, you obviously don't want to tell me. How'd you fancy a proper meal, bed for the night?"

"Where – the police station?"

"No." Mickey shook his head. "I'm not going to turn you in. You can stay at my place a couple of days if you like."

"The caravan?"

"Sure."

"Is it yours? I mean – there's nobody else about?"

Mickey grinned. "Just me and Raider. It's my dad's van but he's away a lot."

The boy shrugged. "Sounds great. Thanks.

I'm Victor, by the way. Call me Vic."

"Mickey," said Mickey. "Raider you met already." He dropped his weapon and wiped his palms down the sides of his jeans. "Come on then – I'll get you that meal I mentioned."

CHAPTER 6

HOSTELS NOW AND THEN

Washed and fed and with the sky full of stars, Vic relaxed enough to sit on the step with Mickey and talk. Raider wasn't sure about him yet, but Mickey made the dog lie down and be quiet.

"What does your dad do?" asked Vic.

Mickey shrugged. "Buys and sells. He's what's known as a general trader."

"Right. So where is he?"

"Search me. Up north I think. Why?"

"Just curious. Seems funny, you living here by yourself. How old are you?"

"Eleven. How about you?"

"Fourteen. Where's your mother?"

"She left when I was little. Where're *your* folks?"

It was Vic's turn to shrug. "I never knew my

dad. My mum's somewhere in London, I think. I've been in care since I was a nipper and I got fed up, ran away."

Mickey looked at him. "Where to?"

"Around. I've been to lots of places."

"What about school?"

Vic laughed. "Haven't seen the inside of a school for two years."

"Where'd you get money, then? For grub and that."

"Odd jobs. Tapping mostly."

"Tapping?"

"Yeah. You know – begging."

"Ah. And where'd you sleep?"

"Doorways, subways. Hostels now and then."

Mickey pulled a face. "Sounds rough."

Vic nodded. "That's why I fell for it, I suppose."

"Fell for what?"

He shook his head. "Doesn't matter. Look – d'you mind if I get my head down now? I'm shattered."

Mickey dug out a sleeping bag and in less than ten minutes the older boy was snoring on Dad's bed. Mickey washed the dishes and tidied up the van. It was ten o'clock. "Well, boy," he said to Raider, stretching and yawning, "might as well get an early night ourselves." He couldn't help wondering what sort of people Vic was running from and whether they were nearby, but Raider would give ample warning if anybody approached, and Dad's shotgun was in the cupboard by his bed. He turned out the light, snuggled down between the sheets and fell asleep. Above the wood the wind blew rags of cloud across the moon, which sailed towards the dawn.

CHAPTER 7

ADVICE

"Givenham Keep, is it?" Farmer Denton poured himself coffee and buttered a slice of toast. "It was known as The Manor when I was a lad. Some poor old geezer lived there alone. Folks reckoned he was barmy, but he was probably just a recluse."

"What's a recluse?" asked Titch, scooping the last spoonful of milk from her cereal bowl.

"Somebody who prefers his own company. Or *her* own – some recluses are women. Anyway, he died when I was about eighteen and the place has been empty ever since, till now."

"What *I'd* like to know," said the farmer's wife, "is why the new owner's got dogs and wire and steel gates all over the place. Has he something to hide, or what?"

The farmer shrugged. "None of our business really, is it?" He looked at Jillo over the rim of his cup. "None of *your* business either, young woman. The Outfit's taken a look at the place which is no more than I'd expect, but you're *not* to go poking your noses in where they're not wanted. The owner wouldn't have gone to the trouble and expense of putting up gates and fences if he wanted company, and he might not be pleased if he sees a bunch of kids snooping about. I'd stay well away if I were you."

"But what if he's a *criminal*?" protested Titch. "Isn't it our *duty* to watch out for criminals, Dad?"

Mr Denton smiled. "He's *not* a criminal, Matilda, and anyway, nobody expects children of your age to go chasing criminals. We have a police force for that sort of work."

"I'm *not* a child," growled Titch. "I'm nearly eight, and Mickey's eleven – practically grown up."

"Matilda." There was a warning note in her mother's voice. "Stop arguing and finish your breakfast. If there's something amiss at Givenham Keep, then we shall know all about it in due course." She smiled. "Nobody can keep a secret for long in a village like Lenton. Too many busybodies."

Breakfast over, the two girls set off to call for Mickey. Titch kicked a pebble. "So that's that. We can't help Mickey and Shaz spy on the mystery owner of Givenham Keep."

Jillo looked at her. "Why not?" They didn't make us promise, Titch. They offered advice, that's all. Where would The Outfit be if it always took advice?"

Titch shrugged. "Dunno."

"Nowhere," growled her sister, "that's where. We solve mysteries because we *don't* do what grown-ups think kids should do. That's the secret of our success."

"Ah-ha." Titch nodded, but Jillo could tell by her voice she hadn't been listening. The caravan was in sight and Titch pointed. "Here's a mystery for you, Jillo – who's that with Mickey?"

CHAPTER 8

CRAZY

"It's okay, Vic – they're friends of mine." The older boy had retreated to the edge of the trees when he'd seen the two girls approaching. He came forward cautiously as Mickey said, "The big one's Jillo, and the little one's Titch. Girls, meet Vic. He's on the run."

"Thanks a lot, Mickey." Jillo could tell by his tone that the boy wished Mickey hadn't said that, but it didn't stop Titch asking, "Who're you running from, Vic?"

Vic smiled faintly and shook his head. "You don't want to know, kid."

"I'm not a kid," corrected Titch. "I thought we might be able to help, that's all."

The big boy shook his head again. "Mickey helped with grub and a night's kip. Now I'm outa here."

31

"Wait – this minute?"

"You *bet* this minute." The boy glanced over his shoulder. "They'll have been out looking since first light and they've got dogs. Tracker dogs." He looked at Mickey. "If they come here you haven't seen me, right?" He clutched at Mickey's sleeve. "Right?"

Mickey jerked his arm free. "Sure. We won't give you away, Vic. We're The Outfit. D'you need anything – money?"

Vic nodded. "Dosh. Yeah – I need dosh all right. Who doesn't?"

"Well, here." Mickey fished in his jeans

pocket. "It's only one pound forty but it's better than nothing." He looked at the sisters. "You got anything?"

Jillo and Titch had fifty-five pence between them. They handed it over. Vic smiled. "Thanks. Thanks a lot. I mean it. You've saved my life." He looked away, then back. "Look – I don't want to tell you what to do, but it sounds like you're some sort of team – The Outfit, was it? Well – stay away from that place, okay? There's nothing you can do, so stay away. That guy – that Orfanoff – he's crazy. He'll do you in as soon as look at you, right? Stay away."

"What place?" cried Mickey, "and who the heck's—?" But before he could complete his question, he and the girls had the clearing to themselves. Vic had vanished between the trees.

CHAPTER 9

ROUGH-LOOKING GUYS WITH A DOG

"So what's been going on?" demanded Jillo as she wiped the breakfast dishes Mickey had washed.

"How'd you get mixed up with this Vic character, and where's he run away from?"

Mickey shrugged. "Me and Raider found him in the van, looking for food. As to where he's running from, your guess is as good as mine."

"My guess is Givenham Keep," countered Jillo promptly.

Mickey smiled. "I thought it might be. So's mine."

"And this guy he mentioned," put in Titch. "Orfanoff. You think he's the one—"

"Who's moved into the old place?" Mickey

nodded. "Yes, Titch, I do. Look – let's wait till Shaz gets here, then have a meeting at HQ. No point going over everything twice."

It was after nine when Shaz showed up. "Hey," he said, "you'll never guess what."

"Your grandad's sending you to join your mum and dad?" suggested Jillo. Shaz's parents were on a long holiday in Pakistan. He grinned. "I wish. No. I got stopped just now by two big, rough-looking guys with a dog. A Doberman. Asked me if I'd seen a tall, thin lad."

"The *Doberman* asked you that?" goggled Titch.

"No, you turkey – the *guys* asked me." He looked at Mickey. "They didn't mean *you*, did they?"

Mickey shook his head. "No, Shaz, but they probably meant a friend of mine. Of ours."

"Really?" Shaz's eyes widened. "Why – have I missed something?"

"We all have," Jillo told him, "except Mickey. There's a meeting at HQ to talk about it."

"When?"

"Now. We were waiting for you."

Outfit HQ had a long table with six chairs, an iron stove with a kettle, and a basket for the dog. There were maps on the walls and rugs on the floor. Raider ignored his basket and sat on one of the chairs. This was a meeting, and Raider always attended meetings.

"Right," said Mickey, when they were all seated. "I've got a story to tell. It's about Vic, the lad Shaz's guys were looking for. I *think* it's about Givenham Keep as well, though I can't prove it, and it *could* add up to a job for The Outfit."

"I hope so!" cried Titch.

Shaz nodded. "So do I."

"Me, too," murmured Jillo. "Six weeks is a long time if there's nothing to do."

"Yip!" agreed Raider, making everybody chuckle. Mickey ruffled the lurcher's coat and began at the beginning.

CHAPTER 10

A REALLY PROMISING START

"So that's it," said Mickey when his tale was told. "The haunted house gets a mysterious buyer who christens it Givenham Keep and turns it into a fortress. We hear dogs in the grounds. A few hours later Vic turns up. He's run away from somewhere. He mentions dogs, and warns us to stay away from *that place*. He doesn't name it, but it *must* be somewhere nearby if he thought we might go there. Then Shaz meets two guys with a dog, looking for a lad. They obviously meant Vic."

He looked around the table. "The way I see it, something's going on at Givenham Keep. Something bad. Now, we *know* we can't get inside, so what I suggest is this: we keep watch by the gates whenever we can, and we start asking questions in the village. *Somebody* must know something about this guy Orfanoff. He bought the house. He had work done on it. He has to eat."

Jillo nodded. "Sounds sensible to me. We can do the village in the daytime and the gates at night. If something funny *is* going on, it's likely they'll operate at night."

"You're right," said Shaz, "and since it's difficult for you and Titch to be out at night, Mickey and I could split the watch between us."

"Hey, hang on!" protested Titch. "We want a share of the excitement too, you know."

"Don't worry, Titch," grinned Mickey. "You'll be called in the minute anything important happens. I've a feeling it'll take all four of us to crack this one."

"Ruff!" went Raider. Mickey looked at him. "All *five* of us, I should've said. Right." He stood up. "Kettle on, cuppa tea, then off to the village." He rubbed his hands together. "I think these holidays are off to a really promising start."

CHAPTER 11

BRILL IDEA

"I know," said Shaz as they entered High Street. "We could ask Linda Fellgate."

Mickey looked at him. "Who?"

"Linda Fellgate. You know – the reporter who got us into the *Echo* just before Jillo was—"

"Oh, yeah – *that* Linda Fellgate." Mickey punched Shaz in the arm.

"Brill idea, Shaz. You go while the rest of us try the shops and stuff."

The offices of the *Lenton Echo* boasted the only revolving door in the village. Shaz got it going and whizzed round three times for fun before sauntering across to the counter. Behind the counter stood a plump woman with folded arms and scarlet lipstick. She glared at Shaz.

"That door is a *door*, not a roundabout," she snapped. "What d'you want?"

"Linda Fellgate," Shaz told her.

"Hrumph!" went the woman. "Miss Fellgate – *Miss* Fellgate is very busy. Have you got an appointment?"

"No."

"Then I'm afraid you can't see her."

"She's a friend," said Shaz. "She'll let me talk to her if you say it's Shaz, of The Outfit."

"Shaz of the *what*?"

"The Outfit. Linda knows us. Try her – please?"

"Just a minute."

The woman went into a poky office. Shaz heard her on the phone, then she came out with a sickly smile on her face. "You can go up," she said. "Second floor. The lift's over there."

Shaz grinned. "First a roundabout, then a lift. Must be my flipping birthday."

When the whizzing door hurled him on to the street fifteen minutes later, there was a broad grin on Shaz's face. He looked for the others and saw Jillo coming out of the barber's shop. "Hey, Jillo!" The girl turned and waited for him. "I think I've got something."

Jillo nodded. "So have I. Mr Orfanoff likes to keep his hair short and so do some of his friends. Let's find Titch and Mickey."

CHAPTER 12

BANANA FINGERS

They went to the Green and sat on a bench near the duck pond. Mickey wouldn't let Raider terrorize the ducks, so he lay under the bench with his head on his paws, sulking.

Mickey looked at Shaz. "So what did Linda Fellgate have to say?"

Shaz grinned. "Plenty. The guy at Givenham Keep is called Rippon Orfanoff. He's in the electronics business – computers and that. He used to have a small factory up north somewhere. Givenham's, it was called. I didn't understand all the stuff Linda told me, but what it comes down to is this. Orfanoff would buy electronic components from the big computer companies, assemble 'em at his factory and sell the finished computers back to the companies. Now Linda says there's *lots* of factories where they do that, but Givenham's could do it *loads* cheaper than anybody else, so Orfanoff got more and more work and the others got less and less. In the end he was getting so much work that the factory wasn't big enough, and *that's* why he moved here and bought the haunted house. It's his new factory."

"And *that's* why he calls it Givenham Keep," said Titch.

Shaz nodded. "That's right."

"And that's why he has wire and gates and all that," mumbled Mickey. "To guard a boring old factory. And we thought—"

"Yeah, but just a minute," interrupted Shaz. "When I told Linda about Vic she gave me a funny look and said, 'Hmmm – that might explain how—'"

"How what?" asked Jillo.

Shaz shrugged. "I dunno. She broke off, and when I asked what she'd been going to say she said, 'Oh, nothing. Doesn't matter'." He grinned. "I *still* think there's something funny going on, and I reckon Linda does too."

Mickey pulled a face. "I dunno. How about you, Jillo – what did you find out?"

"Only that our Mr Orfanoff has hired the

three biggest thugs in Lenton to work for him."

"Who?"

"The Norris boys, as Dad calls them. Morris, Boris and Horace. Morris used to be a wrestler, Boris was a bouncer at a nightclub in town and Horace did a strong-man act round the clubs. Now what use would three guys like *that* be in a computer factory?"

"Heavy lifting?" suggested Shaz.

"Doubt it," said Mickey. "Computers aren't that heavy."

"Somebody's got to do the actual assembling," pointed out Titch.

"I don't suppose Orfanoff does it all himself."

"No, but the *Norris* boys?" Jillo shook her head. "They've got banana fingers, Titch. They couldn't assemble Lego, never mind computers."

"So who *does* assemble 'em?" mused Mickey. "Do you know anybody in Lenton who's got a job at Givenham Keep – apart from the Norris boys, I mean?"

"He might have brought his workers from this place up north," suggested Titch.

"Yeah, but – where *are* they?" asked Mickey. "I mean, we'd see 'em around, wouldn't we?

When they weren't working? Orfanoff can't keep 'em locked up twenty-four hours a day, can he? They'd come to the pub. The shops. They'd need haircuts."

"Vic's hair wasn't so good," murmured Titch. "And I reckon *he'd* been locked up."

"Hey!" Shaz looked at Jillo. "These Norris boys. Are they sort of square, with big shoulders and long arms? Have they got ginger hair?"

Jillo nodded. "That sounds like them. Why?"

"Because it was them I saw with the Doberman. Two of them, anyway."

"Ah-ha." Mickey leaned forward and grinned along the bench.

"Are you guys beginning to think what *I'm* beginning to think?"

"You *bet* we are!" cried the three in unison.

"Yip!" said Raider, coming out of his sulk.

"That's settled then," smiled Mickey. "Come on – this is *definitely* a job for The Outfit."

CHAPTER 13

FACE LIKE A SLOTH

Stay away from that place, Vic had warned. Well, they couldn't do that, but they could be careful, and they were. They left Raider at home for a start. It wouldn't do to get those guard dogs going again. And they didn't go right along to the gates. They stopped at the corner, where tree-shadows and high walls provided cover. If anybody came or went they would see them from here.

Mickey and Titch had bought a bag of plums in the village. The four children sat in long grass, which hid them from the road, eating plums and keeping an eye on the gateway. It was a still, hot afternoon, and when all the plums were gone they began to drowse. Mickey was actually asleep when Shaz hissed, "Listen – is that a motor?"

"Huh – what?" Mickey gazed blearily at his friend.

"A motor."

Jillo nodded. "You're right, Shaz, and it's getting closer. Down, everybody."

They lay on their stomachs and peered through the grassheads. The engine noise grew louder, and presently an old Transit van came lurching along the neglected road. It was going quite slowly, and as it passed their hiding place the children could see that the driver was a bulky woman with a tiny, squashed-up nose. Beside her, a fat boy with exactly the same nose gazed out of his window, seeming to look straight at them. As the vehicle bounced away towards the gates, they saw two other faces pressed against its grimy rear windows. Thin faces and pale, with long greasy hair and red-rimmed eyes.

"Hmmm," went Mickey. "What d'you make of *that*?" The Transit had turned into the gateway and stopped. The driver sounded the horn.

"Didn't like the look of that kid," said Titch. "Face like a sloth."

"I bet the driver's his mum," grinned Shaz.

"They're practically identical."

"It's the two in the back *I'm* worried about," murmured Jillo. "They looked like they wished they were somewhere else, if you know what I mean."

The children couldn't see the steel gates from here but they must have opened, because the Transit rolled forward and disappeared.

"Well," grunted Mickey, "it's a bit late for 'em to wish *that*. They're in now, and I bet they got in a lot easier than they'll get out. He looked at his watch. "Teatime anyway. Who's going and who's staying?"

"I can stay till about nine," volunteered Shaz. "My grandad won't expect me much before then."

Mickey nodded. "Okay. The rest of us'll go, and I'll come back at nine and relieve you when Raider's had his walk. Come on, girls."

The trio stood up, knocking grass seeds off their jeans with their palms. Titch handed the bag of plum stones to Shaz and grinned. "Present for you, Shaz."

"Thanks a lot, Titch."

"See you, Shaz."

"Later, Jillo."

"See you around nine then, Shaz."

"Sure will, Mickey."

He wouldn't, though. Not at nine. Not for a long time. If ever.

CHAPTER 14

COME WITH ME

Nothing happened for an hour or so. Shaz sat propped against the wall, chewing a stem of grass and wondering what Mum and Dad were doing right now in Pakistan. It was just before six when he heard a motor start up and the battered Transit came lurching through the gateway and turned in his direction. Shaz flattened himself in the grass to watch it pass. The driver this time was a guy – one of the pair who'd stopped him that morning – and the other one was in the passenger seat. Shaz watched the van dwindle in a haze of exhaust, then sat up and plucked another stem to chew on.

At half past six the Transit reappeared. Shaz bobbed down again. There was nobody in the passenger seat, but as the vehicle passed his hiding place, one of its rear doors swung open and a tattered youth appeared. The youth seemed about to fling himself from the van when a burly figure grabbed him from behind and hauled him back. Shaz saw the lad's legs kicking and heard a shrill cry, then a thick arm reached out and the door slammed. The Transit stopped in the gateway as before, and the driver sounded the horn. Shaz stayed where he was till the van was inside the grounds then got up, shoved the bag of plum stones in his pocket and tackled the wall, determined to see what was happening. It wasn't an easy climb – the cracks between bricks were narrow and mostly filled with cement – but after a minute he was able to hook his fingers over the top and pull himself up.

The van was parked at the foot of a short flight of steps leading to the front door of the house. As Shaz watched, the driver got out, went to the back of the vehicle and opened the doors. A second man appeared, half-carrying the lad he'd just seen now. The youth was struggling but he had no chance against the two men, who hustled him up the steps and into the house. Shaz was about to drop to the ground when his belt was grabbed and a

voice growled, "Gotcha, you nosy little rat." His yelp of terror turned to one of pain as the man gave his belt a savage jerk and he lost his grip, skittering down the face of the wall which skinned his cheek and fingers as he dropped. He fell into the grass and clamped a hand to his torn cheek, but he was hauled to his feet.

"What're you snooping for, eh? What'd you see?"

"N-nothing," choked Shaz. "I didn't see anything, honest." His cheek stung abominably and he could feel blood trickling down his neck.

The man shook him. "Liar! Tell me what you saw."

"A van," gasped Shaz. "Some guys and a lad."

"You seen too much, kid. Come with me."

"No!" Shaz tried to jerk himself free. He felt as though he was going to be sick as he was pushed and dragged towards the gateway. Seeing the gates open to receive him he gathered his tattered wits, thrust a lacerated hand in his pocket, pulled out what lay there and dropped it in the grass. A second later he was inside. Givenham Keep closed its steel jaws behind him, and swallowed.

CHAPTER 15

BLOOD AND PLUM STONES

It was five to nine and when Mickey reached the wall and walked down to the corner. The sun had set, but it was still light once he was out of the trees. He came to where they'd flattened the grass by sitting on it, but Shaz wasn't there. He frowned. Now where the heck—? He glanced all around but there was no sign of his friend. He shrugged. Must've got fed up and gone home, unless he's spending a penny behind a bush somewhere. He waited, leaning against the wall, but after five minutes it was obvious Shaz wasn't going to show up. Mickey shrugged, sighed and sat down with his back to the wall, which still felt warm from the sun.

One, he told himself. I'll stay till one in the morning. If anything's going to happen, it'll have happened by then. He plucked a grass stem and stuck it in his mouth, wishing Raider was here.

The light began to fade. A blackbird sang sleepily, then stopped. A tiny bat flitted along the wall. Mickey spat his disintegrating stem and reached for another, and it was then he saw the blood.

There wasn't much – just a smear on a dock leaf and a couple of beads on a stem, but his heart kicked and he got to his feet. Had something happened to Shaz? It wasn't like him to desert his post. On the other hand the blood might not be human. A stoat might have taken a rabbit here, or an owl a vole. Bit early for owls, but still. He bent and looked on the ground for more blood, but it was almost dark. He straightened up and gazed towards the gateway.

Was it possible they'd captured Shaz, those Norris boys? Wounded him? Dragged him through that gateway? Was he a prisoner in that awful house?

He began moving along the foot of the wall, keeping its shadow. He moved slowly, watching and listening. The least movement, the slightest sound, would send him pelting for the wood, but there was no movement, and no sound. When he reached the gateway there was a brown paper bag in a dusty rut, and when he picked it up there were plum stones inside, and then he knew.

CHAPTER 16

A FAT MAN'S LAUGH

"Found this one on the wall, Mr Orfanoff. Snoopin'."

"Did you now?" The man who gazed up at Shaz from the depths of an enormous armchair was pink and plump, with fishy blue eyes and a little red mouth. He was wearing a long velvet bathrobe and expensive-looking slippers of scarlet suede. His head was bald except for a halo of fine golden fuzz, and the hands that curled over the end of the chair arms were small and soft like a baby's, with dimples instead of knuckles. In fact the total effect was that of a great, sulky baby, bathed and powdered and ready for bed. He nodded. "All right Horace, you can let go now. Wait outside."

"Very good, Sir." Horace released Shaz and shambled from the room, quietly closing the double doors behind him. Man and boy stared at each other.

"What's your name, boy?"

"Shaz."

"That's not a name. What's your *full* name?"

"Shazad Butt, and I wasn't snooping."

The man laughed wheezily, a fat man's laugh. "No? I suppose you shinned up my wall for the exercise?"

"Something like that."

The smile vanished. "I'd advise against impudence, boy. We don't tolerate impudence at Givenham Keep."

"Let me go, then. My mum and dad'll be looking for me."

Orfanoff wheezed again. "They won't look for you *here*."

"They'll get the police."

"*They* won't look here either – why should they?"

"Because of Vic. He'll tell them."

"Vic?" The man looked startled for an instant, then nodded. "So you met our Victor, did you? What a very good thing that Horace found you, Shazad Butt. It might have been – embarrassing, shall we say, if you'd gone spreading Victor's tales in the village." He smiled. "Victor's back with us, by the way. He didn't *want* to return, but my men were able to persuade him, and now he's being punished for his foolish excursion. So you see – he won't be telling the police anything."

"Let me go."

"Sorry – can't be done. You know too much, thanks to poor Victor." Orfanoff turned towards the door. "HORACE!" The door opened at once.

"You called, Sir?"

"Yes. Take this creature away. Put him with the others. He's a poor specimen, but I daresay we'll find something for him to do."

The big man chuckled. "We will, Sir. He'll not be idle long – not with my boot behind him." He grabbed a fistful of Shaz's collar, yanked him off his feet and carried him from the room.

CHAPTER 17

LIKE SOMEONE IN A MOVIE

Mickey stood outside the iron gates, wondering what to do. He felt like picking up a stone to batter the gates with till somebody came, then demanding his friend's release, but he knew it wouldn't work. They'd say Shaz wasn't there, and they'd probably grab him too, and what good would *that* do?

He wished Titch and Jillo were here to help, but it was nearly twenty past nine and quite dark. There was no way Farmer Denton was going to let his daughters out at this time of night. So, he told himself, that leaves two options. Shaz's grandad, or the police, and I reckon grandad should be first. He'll be starting to worry, and he might know what to do next.

Mickey stuffed the bag of plum stones in his pocket and made his way back to the corner and through the wood. It was almost ten o'clock when he reached the village. Shaz's grandad was on his doorstep. Mickey walked up the path.

"Hello, Mr Butt."

"Mickey. Shazad is very late. Have you seen him?"

"No, Mr Butt, I haven't, but I know where he is."

"Tell me, please."

Mickey pulled a face. "Can we go inside? It's a bit dodgy, I'm afraid."

"Dodgy?" The old man peered at him. "What is this dodgy? Has something happened to my grandson?"

"Well, yes, I'm afraid it has."

"Oh, no – Oh, Mickey! His father – what will his father say? I am responsible, you see." He grabbed the boy's sleeve. "He's not...?"

Mickey shook his head. "Not dead, no, but he's been kidnapped."

"*Kidnapped*? But why? Who has done this thing? Oh, I must sit. I am not a well man, Mickey. Help me inside, please."

The old man's legs were so wobbly it was as much as Mickey could do to steer him indoors, where he slumped into an armchair. His hands were shaking. His face, shiny with sweat, looked grey under the electric light.

Mickey regarded him anxiously. "Mr Butt?" The old man mumbled something he didn't catch. "Are you all right, Mr Butt? Can I get you a drink of water?" There was no reply. Mr Butt's head was bowed and his body crumpled as though his bones had suffered some sort of attack. What do I *do*? He glanced about him. There was a phone on the glass-top table under the window. He crossed the room, lifted the handset and punched 999, seeing his reflection in the window. He felt like someone in a movie.

CHAPTER 18

LIKE GHOSTS

Shaz was half dragged, half carried up two flights of stairs. The second flight was steep and narrow with a door at the top. Horace held on to Shaz with one hand and drew three stout bolts with the other. The door creaked open to reveal nothing but darkness.

"Get in," grunted Horace, giving him a shove in the back. Shaz staggered forward, tripped over something he couldn't see and fell. The door slammed and he heard the scrape of the bolts.

"Trample all over me, why don't you?" said a voice in his ear. Shaz jumped, and somebody chuckled. There seemed to be a number of people nearby.

"Who – who is it?" stammered Shaz. "Vic?"

Another chuckle. "Vic's not here. Wishes he

was, I expect." He felt a hand on his sleeve. "Here – sit by me. Your eyes'll get used to it in a bit."

Shaz was sitting on the edge of something soft. A mattress, perhaps. As his eyes adjusted to the darkness he saw a number of pale moving blobs. "I think I can see you now," he murmured. "Like ghosts."

"Aye, that's us all right," said a voice he hadn't heard before. "The ghosts of Givenham Keep. Who're you?"

"Shaz. Shazad Butt."

"How *old're* you, for pete's sake?"

"Ten."

"*Ten!*" Murmurs in the dark. "I *thought* you sounded young. Hear that, guys. He's started taking little kids now."

"Who are you?" asked Shaz. He could make out dim shapes now. Ten or eleven perhaps, sitting or sprawling. "What're you all *doing* here?"

"Us? Oh, we're being saved." Laughter. "Orfanoff saved us from the streets. From unemployment. Gave us a roof over our heads and three square meals a day. Mind you, that's three square meals between eleven of us.

Twelve, now you're here. Oh, and training. Mustn't forget the training."

"Training?" asked Shaz.

"Oh, aye. Job training. You'll get it tomorrow. Takes about ten minutes. After that you'll work. And work. And work. Am I right, lads?"

A chorus of confirmation came out of the gloom. "Better bed down, kid," said the lad he'd tripped over. "Long day tomorrow and we start at six. There's a pile of spare mattresses over there. You hungry?"

"Yes," said Shaz.

"So are we." Their laughter mocked him as he dragged a mattress off the pile and found a bit of floor space.

CHAPTER 19

OVERDEVELOPED IMAGINATIONS

Mickey stood aside as the paramedics stretchered the old man through the door with an oxygen mask clamped to his face. "Ambulance," he'd said when asked which service, and they'd *sent* an ambulance. Trouble was, its crew weren't interested in his story about Shaz. There wasn't time, they'd said. Seconds might be crucial. They slid Mr Butt aboard, slammed the doors and roared off with the blue light flashing and the siren wailing, leaving Mickey to gaze after them from the old guy's doorstep.

What now? He turned and went into the empty house. Can't walk away and leave the place wide open, can I? Keys. He hunted around and found a ring of keys on a table in the hallway. He found the right one by trying them all. He checked that the back door was locked, switched off the TV and lights and left, locking the door and slipping the keys into his pocket. It was twenty past ten.

The police station was in the middle of the village. Mickey ran there and approached the front desk, where Sergeant Hunt was on duty.

"Yes, lad?"

"I've come about my mate, Sergeant. Shazad Butt."

"Oh aye – what about him?"

"He's been kidnapped."

The officer arched his brow. "When, where and by whom?"

"Tonight, outside Givenham Keep. The Norris boys got him."

"How d'you know?"

"I found this." Mickey pulled the bag of plum stones from his pocket and laid it on the counter. The sergeant prodded it and looked inside. "Hmm. A bag of plum stones. Not what I'd call cast-iron proof, son. Where'd you find it?"

"Right outside the gates, Sergeant. There was blood too, on the grass."

"Ah-ha." The sergeant gazed at Mickey.

"Young Wilbury, isn't it – Michael Wilbury?"

"Yes, Sergeant."

"And aren't you in that gang – what d'you call yourselves?"

"The Outfit. Yes, I am."

"Aye, The Outfit. Funny bunch of kids. Overdeveloped imaginations in my opinion." He consulted his watch. "Half-past ten. If this kid's gone missing, I'd have thought his parents would be worried by now, but they haven't been in touch."

"They're away," said Mickey. "Pakistan."

"So who looks after your mate?"

"His grandad."

And isn't *he* worried?"

"Yes. In fact he had a heart attack when I told him. They rushed him into hospital."

"When was this?"

"Ten minutes ago."

"Ah-ha." The sergeant smiled. "And you came and told me so I'd have a heart attack too, is that it?"

"No – it's not *like* that. It happened just as I said."

"I'm sure it did, lad. Sure as my grandad was Count Dracula." He fixed Mickey with a cold stare. "I'd run along now son, if I was you. I've a long night ahead of me, and night duty tends to shorten my temper."

"But – but –"

"No buts. Out, this minute."

Mickey left.

CHAPTER 20

BUMPER

Shaz couldn't sleep. The room was cold, the mattress thin and lumpy. There was no pillow and no bedclothes. Some of the others snored or cried out in their sleep. He was hungry and scared. He lay on his side, curled up, thinking.

Grandad. He'll be out of his skull, worrying. He'll have told the police by now, but what will *they* do? They'll say, I shouldn't worry, sir – he's probably left home. Happens all the time, young kids. He'll be back when he's hungry, you'll see.

Mickey. He came at nine to relieve me and I wasn't there. What did he do? Did he think I'd gone home? Did he look around – find the plum stones? Does he *know* I'm in here? And if he does, will he be able to make anybody believe him?

71

Sleep. I've got to sleep. Long day tomorrow.

Perhaps he dozed. He didn't feel as though he had, but when he opened his eyes the gloom was less thick. He rolled on to his back and saw three small windows in the slope of the roof. They were heavily barred, but the grey light they admitted told Shaz it was almost morning. He groaned and turned on his side.

He must have fallen asleep again, because the next thing he knew there was a loud bang and the attic was full of light and some kid was shouting at the top of his voice. Shaz knuckled his burning eyes and peered towards the sound. The door was wide open. In the doorway stood a fat lad of about fifteen with a baseball bat in his hand. "Come on, you lazy fat pigs!" he hollered, banging the baseball bat against the door frame. "Last man down, no breakfast."

All round, lads were sitting up, stretching and groaning, scrambling to their feet. Shaz spoke to the nearest. "Who's the fat kid?"

The youth snorted. "That's Bumper, and he'd better not hear you call him fat." He stood up. "You'd better shift and all, if you want to eat." Shaz had another question, but before he could spit it out the lad was away, half-running across the bare boards towards the doorway where Bumper stood, tapping the door frame while kids hurried past him, heading for the stairs. They'd slept in their clothes, and in twenty seconds the attic was empty except for Shaz. The fat youth sneered.

"What's up – servant forget to wake you with tea, did he?"

"No – no. I mean – "

"I don't give a monkeys *what* you mean," cried Bumper. "Get your carcass down them steps NOW! You missed breakfast but you ain't missing work, so don't think it." He hit the doorpost with the bat. MOVE!"

Shaz moved.

CHAPTER 21

SERIOUSLY DODGY

Mickey had a poor night and was drinking tea at Outfit HQ when Jillo and Titch arrived at eight thirty.

"*You're* bright and early," chirped Titch. "Looks like we're waiting for Shaz as usual."

"Wish we were," growled Mickey. Briefly, he told them everything that had happened last night.

"So Sergeant Hunt didn't believe you," said Jillo.

"No."

"We could try now – it'll be somebody else on duty."

"Hmmm." Mickey pulled a face. "I dunno, Jillo. I've been sitting here thinking how we might do something ourselves."

"How?" asked Titch. "We can't even get

inside the grounds, and if we *did* we couldn't take on the Norris boys and a pack of savage dogs. We'd end up as prisoners ourselves, or worse."

Mickey drained his tea mug and wiped his mouth with the back of his hand. "There might be a way, Titch. Listen to this and tell me what you think." The girls sat down. Mickey folded his arms on the table and rested his chin on them, wishing he could doze off instead of talking. "I think I can get us into the grounds, but you're right, Titch – once in, we're gonna need help. I was thinking about the fire brigade."

"The fire brigade?" cried Jillo. "How're you gonna get *them* to come?"

"Tell you in a minute," said Mickey. "First we've got to get inside the grounds, and Raider can help us there."

"How?" asked Titch.

"By drawing off the dogs. What we do is climb the wall, snip the wire with my dad's bolt-cutters and put Raider over. He'll bark, the dogs'll chase him and we're in."

Titch chuckled. "Have you asked Raider if he fancies it, Mickey?"

The boy smiled. "He'll do it. The dog isn't born that can get the better of a lurcher. He'll lead 'em a proper dance."

"And then what?" asked Jillo.

"And then we set fire to something."

"What – and hope old Orfanoff calls the fire brigade?"

"No. *We* call the brigade before we put Raider in. The fire's just to make sure they get past the gates."

Jillo pulled a face. "Sounds seriously dodgy to me, Mickey. What do we set fire to? And how do we do it?"

"Yes, and *when* do we do it?" put in Titch. Mickey looked at her. "We do it tonight, Titch. It's *Shaz* they've got in that dump – our mate. Let's do the oath."

"But there's only three of us, Mickey."

"We're The Outfit, Titch," he replied. "We're together, even when we're apart. Come on."

So they did.

CHAPTER 22

BEST FRIENDS

Shaz followed the others down two flights of stairs and found himself last in a queue which was shuffling into a big room. Inside the room were some trestle tables and folding chairs. Behind the first table stood the bulky woman with the squashed up nose he'd seen in the Transit yesterday. She had a ladle that she was using to scoop some sort of grey gunge from the crusted iron pan in front of her and slop it on to plates which the lads had picked up as they filed past. Beyond the pan stood a large aluminium tray stacked with sliced bread. Each boy was grabbing a wad of this with his free hand and carrying his meal to one or other of the tables. The food looked unappetizing to say the least, but Shaz was starving and could hardly contain his impatience at the slowness of the queue. His mouth watered and his tummy rumbled. When there was only one boy in front of him a hand fell on his shoulder and Bumper growled, "Not *you*. You were last. You just get the smell."

"But I'm hungry!" cried Shaz. "I'll work better if—"

The fat boy chuckled. "You'll work pretty good anyway with Boris, Morris and Horace breathing down your neck." He jabbed Shaz between the shoulder blades with his bat. "Move out!"

As Shaz dropped out of line some girls came shuffling through the doorway and formed a queue. They were pale and listless and showed no curiosity as Shaz was hustled by. In passing, Bumper thrust his bat under the chin of the hindmost girl, a frail-looking creature with ginger hair, freckles and granny specs.

"Come on, you," he snarled. "You know the rules."

"But I was last *yesterday*," wailed the girl.

"Too flippin' slow then, ain't cha?" sneered Bumper. "Get up here with him."

Side by side, the pair were prodded along a passage and through a pair of double doors into a very large room with high ceiling and big windows along one side. Shaz saw long benches stacked with circuit boards and small tools and lots of stuff he didn't recognize. A tangled web of cables snaked across the floorboards between stacks of plastic boxes with symbols stencilled on them. Bumper shoved the pair towards the nearest bench.

"Siddown," he grunted. "You." He prodded the girl. "Show him the ropes till the instructors arrive. And no mucking about or there'll be no grub at dinnertime either." He swaggered off.

Shaz looked at the girl. "They can't *do* this," he murmured. "Why don't you rush 'em – all together – break out?"

The girl snorted. "Think it's easy, do you? Think nobody's fought of it before. Forget it, kid. Look." She picked up a tool. "This is a soldering iron. You've got one in front of you. It's your best friend."

Shaz shook his head. "Not *my* best friend. My best friends're out there." He nodded towards the window. "And *they'll* get me out of here, you'll see."

CHAPTER 23

THE OLD RUNAROUND

After lunch, Jillo slipped away while Titch was helping Mum with the washing up. She was seriously worried about Mickey's plan, so she walked into Lenton with a plan of her own. The police hadn't believed Mickey, but they might take notice of Shaz's grandad. She would go to the hospital and get the old man to call them.

It was a good idea, but it didn't work.

"Mr Butt is resting," said the clerk on reception. "He's not allowed visitors – not even family. You could try tomorrow, but phone first to avoid a wasted journey."

"Tomorrow," growled Jillo as she crossed the hospital grounds. "Tomorrow'll be too late, won't it? We could all be *dead* tomorrow." She decided to try the police herself, and hurried along to the station.

A very tall constable stood at the front desk. "Now, Miss, what can we do for you?" he enquired.

Jillo looked at him. "I *know* you'll think I'm making this up, but a friend of mine's being held prisoner at Givenham Keep. His name's Shazad Butt. His grandad's in hospital and there's nobody else to report this. Will you send somebody to investigate, please?"

The constable sighed. "Look Miss, you're the second youngster who's come in here with this kidnap story. Michael Wilbury had no evidence to back it up, and I don't suppose you have either." He shook his head. "It's not like on the telly, you know – we can't go barging into somebody's home just because some kid comes along with a tall story. And besides, your friend Shazad's got a history of wandering off. His grandad's called us several times in the past because the kid hasn't come home at night, and he's always turned up safe and sound. He's probably at home right now, catching up on some sleep."

"He's *not*," cried Jillo. "He's at Givenham Keep. I *know* he is."

She went to the house anyway, just to make

sure. She hammered on the door, peered through the window, called the boy's name. The place was locked up. Empty. She returned to the police station. The same constable was there. "I've tried the house," she said. "He's not there."

The constable sighed again, reaching for a thick ledger. "All right, Miss." He picked up a ballpoint pen. "We'll register him as missing. What's your full name?"

It took twenty minutes to register Shaz as officially missing. When the paperwork was finally done Jillo said, "So you'll search Givenham Keep now?"

The constable shook his head. "I doubt it, Miss. No evidence, you see."

"Then what *are* you going to do?"

The policeman closed the ledger. "I think you can safely leave that to us, Miss. We'll be in touch with the grandfather if there are developments."

Developments, brooded Jillo as she trudged along the street. There'll be developments all right, only *you* won't be there to see 'em. She kicked an empty drink carton into the gutter. It's like Dad says. You can never find a policeman when you need one.

She was halfway home when she thought of Linda Fellgate.

CHAPTER 24

CARCASSES

"This is a carcass," said the freckled girl. She showed Shaz a grey plastic box, open at one end. "And this is a circuit board. What you do is, you take these three wires sticking out of the carcass and solder 'em onto the circuit board here, here and here. Make sure they're firmly attached, then shove the board into the carcass so that it engages these two clips. Make sure you shove it in the right way up. When you've done that, you pass the whole thing to the kid on your left and grab another carcass and board from me. You do that all day, you do it fast, and you do it right. These PCs are inspected before they go out. Any fault, Orfanoff knows exactly who did it, and you get no grub for twenty-four hours. Okay?"

Shaz shook his head. "No, it's *not* okay – er,

what's your name?"

"Midge."

"It's not okay, Midge. It's slavery, and slavery's not *allowed* any more."

Midge chuckled. "Orfanoff's not bothered what's allowed, kid. He makes his own rules. You step out of line and you'll have Boris, Morris and Horace after you. Not to mention Bumper. He's Orfanoff's son, by the way. He's supposed to go to school but he never does. And then there's his mum, Carrie-Anne. She's in charge of us girls, and she's awful. She – look out, here they come."

The other kids were coming through the doorway, shepherded by Bumper and two of the Norris boys. Each kid moved quickly to a seat and sat down. There was a momentary pause while the two men counted them, then a buzzer sounded and they jerked into motion, grabbing parts from stacks at their sides, putting them together and passing them on. Midge shoved a carcass and board at Shaz, who fumbled with the wires, aware that the boy on his left was waiting.

A shadow fell across the bench and a voice growled, "Not like *that*, you dummy. Like *this*." Boris's fingers were surprisingly nimble for a man of his size. In seconds the connections were made, the board clicked into place and Boris shoved the carcass at Shaz's neighbour before seizing Shaz's ear and twisting it. "*That's* how it's done, kid," he hissed. "Now get on with it." The shadow withdrew.

Without looking at him, Midge slid another set his way and whispered, "That was your training. Good, eh?"

It wasn't good. Shaz fumbled, trying to go too fast. Boards and carcasses piled up on his right while the boy on his left, scared of missing his dinner, muttered, "Come on, you dummy, come *on*." He dropped a board on the floor, burned his hand with the hot iron and ran a wire under his fingernail which bled, leaving smudges on everything he touched. The room grew hot. Airless. Shaz's throat became parched. Why didn't they open a window? Bring water? Do we ever get a break?

"What time is it?" he croaked, after what seemed like hours.

"About half-seven," hissed Midge.

"Is that *all*?" At home, he'd just be getting up. "When do we...?"

"Eleven," murmured Midge. "Lavatories and water at eleven, then on till six." She chuckled drily. "Where are these friends of yours anyway – I thought you said they'd be along to get you out?"

"They will," grunted Shaz, swallowing hard to keep from bursting into tears. "They will."

CHAPTER 25

I DON'T THINK THAT'S WISE

Linda Fellgate gazed at Jillo across her cluttered desk. "So you're pretty sure Shaz is being held at Givenham Keep?"

Jillo nodded. "Dead sure. He's *never* stayed away this long, and besides there were the plum stones, right in the gateway."

"Hmmm." The reporter steepled her fingers and rested her chin on them. "And The Outfit's going to attempt a rescue?"

"Yes."

"Tonight?"

"Yes."

"I don't think that's wise, Jillo."

"Neither do I. That's why I came to you. I was hoping you might think of another way. A less dangerous way."

Linda Fellgate pulled a face. "I'm sorry, but

I don't think I can. If what we both suspect is true, it's a job for the police, but they *do* need evidence, Jillo. A bag of plum stones just isn't enough."

"So you can't help?"

"I don't know. You'll have to let me think about it. Will you go with them tonight on this...rescue?"

"Oh, yes. They rescued *me* once, you see. And anyway, we're The Outfit."

The reporter smiled. "Of course you are." She stood up. "I ought to try and stop you but I won't. Just be careful, and I'll have a think and try to find a way to help."

Jillo grinned. "I know you will. See you tonight, then."

"Lenton 646342."

"Is that Givenham Keep?"

"Uh – yeah. Who's calling?"

"Why do you ask?"

"Uh – I gotta get a name before I put you through, Miss."

"I don't *want* you to put me through. Your name's Norris, isn't it?"

"Y–yeah, that's right."

"Then my call is for you."

"For *me*? Who – who are you? Whaddya want with me?"

"Let's just say I'm a friend. You know you're in big trouble, don't you – you and your brothers?"

"Trouble? What trouble? What you on about?"

"I'm on about the kids, Mr Norris. Victor and Shazad and the others."

"Kids? I don't know noffing about kids."

"Ah, but *I* do, Mr Norris, and so do the police. They're coming. Tonight. Surprise raid. If I were you, I'd get myself and my brothers out of there the minute it gets dark. Why should *you* go to prison for Mr Orfanoff's crimes?"

"*Prison*? I'm not off to prison. I didn't snatch no kids. I only work here."

"*I* know that, Mr Norris, but the police don't. Tell your brothers. Nobody else. Wait till dark, then go."

"Why you telling me this? Who *are* you?"

"I told you – a friend. I've got to hang up now. Get out quick, and good luck."

"Hello? Are you still there? Hel—"

CHAPTER 26

BLUE FLAME

It was ten to nine and dusk when Mickey punched 999 on his dad's mobile phone. He, Titch and Jillo crouched in bushes a few feet from the wall they'd shortly scale. Raider lay beside them, his tongue lolling. Jillo gripped a plastic can full of paraffin and Titch had a long, heavy wirecutter.

"Fire, please." Mickey winked at them. "Oh – I want to report a fire at Givenham Keep. No, not the house – a shed. Long wooden shed just inside the gates. It's well alight by the look of it. No, I was passing and saw smoke. I don't know – they mustn't have noticed. I banged on the gates and shouted, but nobody came. Er– Wilbury. Michael Wilbury. Thanks. 'Bye."

"They're on their way. Come on!" The four rose and dashed to the foot of the wall.

Jillo bent over and Titch helped Mickey on to her sister's back. "Cutter," he rapped. Titch passed the tool and he reached up, snipping the first strand. It parted with a ping and coiled away, its end hanging like steel vines down the brickwork. The second and third strands were disposed of in the same way, leaving a gap two metres wide in the Keep's defences.

Mickey dropped the cutter and hissed, "Raider! Here boy." As the dog leapt on Jillo's back Mickey grabbed his collar and a fistful of the coarse hair on his back and boosted him. Claws scrabbled on brick as the dog's hind legs sought purchase on the smooth face of the wall. A volley of barking erupted from somewhere inside the grounds. "Go get 'em, Raider!" A final shove and the dog was up and over, yipping his challenge as he streaked between the trees.

"Paraffin!" cried Mickey. No point in silence now. Speed was all. Titch passed up the can and Mickey put it on top of the wall. "Okay Titch – now you." He pulled her up and steadied her till she straddled the wall, then hauled himself up. "C'mon, Jillo." He reached down. Jillo had straightened up and was massaging the small of her back with both hands.

"Felt like a herd of elephants climbing on me," she gasped. She put her hands in Mickey's and scrabbled with her trainers as he pulled her aloft.

They sat for a moment, gazing into the gloom. There was a lot of barking and snarling but it was some way off, and there was no sign of movement between the trees.

"Good old Raider!" grinned Mickey. "Here we go."

The grass was long under the trees. As the trio scampered along under the wall, heading for the long wooden shed near the gates, they heard sirens in the distance. "Here come the fire brigade!" cried Titch.

There was nobody near the shed. "This is amazing," panted Mickey. "The Norris boys must be asleep. Keep a lookout anyway." He unscrewed the cap and splashed paraffin on the shed's planking. The sirens swelled. Blue light strobed treetops beyond the wall. When he had wet a large area, Mickey threw the can aside, fumbled a matchbox from his pocket, struck a match and flicked it at the wall. The paraffin whooshed into blue flame, which climbed the shed, licking at the felted roof. The sirens were deafening now and the barking continued, but nobody came running. Jillo wondered fleetingly whether Linda Fellgate had something to do with their good fortune.

CHAPTER 27

SAVE ME, MAM

"Hey, listen." In the dim attic dormitory, conversation ceased as the youths turned to peer at Shaz.

Vic, released at last from the black, airless cupboard they'd crammed him into after his recapture, said, "What's up, kid?"

"Sssh!" Shaz, head on one side, strained his ears.

"It's just the dogs," growled Vic. "After a rabbit."

"No." Shaz shook his head. "It *is* the dogs, but there's something else. I think I heard Raider."

"Raider? You mean the dog that—?"

"Flushed you out of your tree, yes." Shaz was on his feet now, under one of the barred skylights. Out there in the grounds the

95

Dobermans were going mad, but through their frantic barking he could hear a high-pitched yipping, which he knew could only be Raider. "It *is* him," he cried, "and if Raider's here, so are the others."

Vic rose stiffly to his feet and joined Shaz under the skylight. The other lads continued to sit or sprawl on their mattresses, but nobody spoke. All eyes were on that twilit rectangle in the slope of the roof. As they listened, a siren wailed in the distance.

Shaz looked at Vic. "Police?"

The thin youth shrugged. "Could be. Long way off, though."

They listened as the siren faded, swelled and faded again.

"Naw," growled Vic. "Not coming here."

"I dunno," contradicted Shaz. "I think it's getting closer." He glanced at the darkening sky. "What's that?"

Vic gripped two of the bars and went up on his toes. Light flickered somewhere.

"Looks like – like something's on fire." He turned. "The siren. It's a fire engine. I can smell burning. I think the flipping house is on fire!"

They youths scrambled to their feet. They'd

imagined this a hundred times – the house burning and themselves locked up here. Trapped. One boy ran to the door. "Help!" he yelled. "Let us out." He rattled the knob and battered the oak with his fists.

"Don't waste your breath," cried Vic. "If the place is going they'll *want* us dead so we can't grass 'em up. *Kick* it as hard as you can. Try near the lock. Keep kicking. Somebody give me a hand with these flipping bars."

They battered the door, smashed the glass in the skylights and wrenched at the bars, yelling at the tops of their voices. With the glass gone the siren was louder, the reek of burning more distinct. In their room across the landing, the girls had realized what was happening and were pounding their own door. In a murky corner, Midge dug her nails into a floorboard she'd been working on for months, lifted it and threw it to one side. Thrusting her leg into the gap, she began kicking at the lath and plaster between the two joists. A crack appeared in the ceiling of the bedroom below. Plaster-dust drifted down. Carrie-Anne Orfanoff woke, coughed and rolled off the bed, spitting plaster.

"Oi!" she screeched, staggering towards

the door. "What the studbusted rumplepoop's going on up there?" Intent on punishing her prisoners she wrenched open the door.

Outside was Bumper. He flung his arms round her. "Mam!" he wailed. "Save me, Mam. The Norris boys have gone, the warehouse is ablaze and a fire engine's rammed the gates."

Carrie-Anne broke her son's grip and knocked his fat arms away. "Geroff me, you useless tub of lard. Where's your dad?"

"He's in the van," choked Bumper. "He sent me to get you. Said he'd wait ten seconds, then go. Come *on*, Mam!" There was a crash from inside the room. Bumper looked over his mother's shoulder and saw a thin leg dangling from the ceiling. Midge had broken through.

CHAPTER 28

I KNEW YOU'D COME

The shed was half-consumed when the firefighters gave up trying to attract attention and burst through the steel gates with their machine. As they leapt down and began running out the hoses, they found themselves hampered by three children who appeared out of nowhere, yelling and pointing towards the house.

"The house is okay," grunted a sweating fireman. "It's the shed we've got to save."

"Kids!" croaked Jillo, her throat full of smoke. "They've got kids in there. Prisoners."

"Don't talk daft." The hose was heavy. Struggling to twist its nozzle, the man looked like someone wrestling a python.

Jillo planted herself in front of him. "I'm *not* talking daft!" she yelled. "It was us that *called*

99

you. We started the fire. Look." She waved the plastic can in his face. Paraffin sloshed about in the bottom. "They've got our friend in there. We had to rescue him somehow so we called you and lit up the shed. That's our dog you can hear, sorting out the Dobermans."

The firefighter looked at Jillo, then at the shed. "*You* did this?"

"Uh-ha."

"On purpose, to get us here?"

"Yep."

"But you – don't you know that's a very serious offence? You can go to *jail* for that."

"This is jail," choked Jillo. "Forget the rotten shed and look in the house, *please*!"

A second firefighter loomed. "What's the trouble, Perkins? Why's that hose not deployed?"

"Sir – this kid says she started the fire to get us here. She says kids are being held prisoner in the house. You better talk to her, sir."

The man turned to Jillo, but before he could open his mouth they heard the sound of an engine and the Transit bounced past at speed, heading for the ruined gates.

"That's him!" cried Jillo. "Rippon Orfanoff.

He *owns* this dump."

Hunched over the wheel, Orfanoff aimed his vehicle at the gap between the gates. He'd almost made it when a police car nosed into the opening and stopped, its blue light flashing. Orfanoff baled out of the van and found himself confronted by two uniformed officers. "Just a minute, sir, if you don't mind," said Sergeant Hunt. "We'd like to ask you a few questions."

"Ask him, where Shaz is!" cried Mickey. "You wouldn't believe *me*."

After that it was only a matter of time. A second car arrived. Four officers and two firefighters went inside the house. The firefighters had axes. The children watched by the light of the blazing shed. After a minute, two of the officers emerged with Carrie-Anne and her son. Bumper was weeping. The officers helped the pair into the back of the car. Rippon was in the other.

Splintering crashes from the house were followed by the sound of youngsters cheering. Seconds later they came streaming through the doorway and down the steps – thin youths and ragged girls, their gaunt features ruddy in

the glow of the fire. Last out, just in front of the police and firefighters, was Shaz. He stood blinking on the top step as Jillo, Titch and Mickey ran yelling down the drive towards him.

"The Outfit's here!" cried Titch, bounding up the steps and flinging herself into his arms. Shaz hugged her as the others closed in, slapping him on the back and ruffling his hair.

He smiled through his tears. "I *knew* you'd come," he said.

CHAPTER 29

A FRIEND

They didn't meet for three days and when they did, Shaz didn't show up till eleven.

"About time," growled Mickey. "We were beginning to think we'd never see you again."

"I've been to visit Grandad," said Shaz. "He's out of danger. He'll be coming home next week and I'm glad: I don't know how you stand it by yourself, Mickey."

Mickey nodded. "That's great, Shaz. He nearly scared me to death when he had that funny turn." He grinned. "So we're *all* out of danger."

Shaz nodded. "Including the ghosts of Givenham Keep."

Titch looked at him. "Who?"

"The ghosts of Givenham Keep," repeated Shaz. "That's what one of the lads called the prisoners."

"Ah." Titch smiled. "They're out of danger *and* in work, Shaz."

"How'd you mean?"

Titch looked at her sister. "Shall I tell 'em, or will you?"

"You," smiled Jillo. "I know you're dying to."

"You're right, I *am*." She looked at the boys. "Dad told us at breakfast that a pal of his who grows salads under glass – cucumbers and tomatoes and lettuces and stuff – is expanding his business. He's built some new glasshouses and a packaging plant, and he's taking on *all* Orfanoff's kids to work for him. They'll get proper wages and a decent place to sleep."

"That's fantastic!" cried Mickey. "I can't *believe* how everything's worked out. I mean, nobody tried to stop us when we went into the grounds. Raider escaped without a scratch because the Dobermans were fastened up in their run. The police arrived just as the firefighters were getting ready not to believe us, and now this. It's as if somebody *fixed* it all."

"Somebody up there likes us, Mickey," smiled Shaz. "That's what it is."

"Yeah, well—" Mickey broke off as

somebody knocked on the door. "Who is it?"

"Only me," said a woman's voice. "Linda from the *Echo*. I hear The Outfit scored another triumph. May I come in?"

"Sure," said Mickey, jumping up to open the door. Nobody noticed the flush on Jillo's cheeks. The reporter came in. There was no spare chair, so Mickey gave her his, and busied himself with teapot and kettle.

"Well." She smiled at the faces round the table. "I was wondering if you'd mind giving me your story?"

"Yip!" said Raider.

Mickey turned. "Quiet, you rude hound," he admonished. "We haven't forgotten how you pretended to be fighting those Dobermans when they were locked in their run all the time." He looked at the reporter. "Of course we don't mind. We *love* reading about ourselves in the paper, don't we folks?" The others grinned and nodded, except Raider, who only grinned.

Linda smiled. "Good. I understand you have a little ritual you perform before you set out on your investigations – a sort of oath. Is that right?"

"Right," confirmed Shaz.

"Well, I'd like to see you do it if that's all right."

"Hmmm." Mickey put the teapot on the table and went to get the mugs. "It's secret actually," he said. "Members only, but I suppose we could make an exception for a friend." He poured tea. "You *are* a friend, aren't you?"

Linda smiled briefly, a secret smile. "Oh, I'm a friend all right – ask the Norris boys."

Mickey looked at her. "What?"

"Oh, nothing," said the reporter innocently. "It was nothing, Mickey. Let's hear the famous oath."

"Okay." The children pushed back their chairs. Raider jumped down from his. They squatted in a circle with the dog in the middle.

"Faithful, fearless, full of fun," they chanted.
"Winter, summer, rain or sun,
One for five and five for one –
THE OUTFIT!"

On the last word they leapt in the air with their arms raised, breaking the circle. "YIP!" went Raider. It was time for tea.

READ ALL OF THE OUTFIT'S THRILLING ADVENTURES!

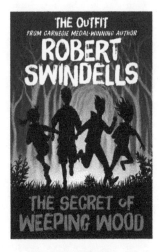

ISBN 978-1-78270-053-1

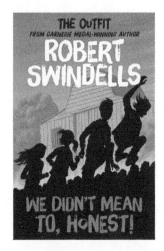

ISBN 978-1-78270-054-8

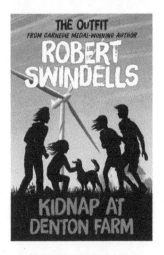

ISBN 978-1-78270-055-5

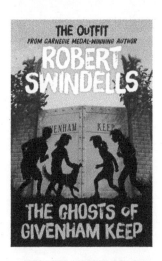

ISBN 978-1-78270-056-2

READ ALL OF THE OUTFIT'S THRILLING ADVENTURES!

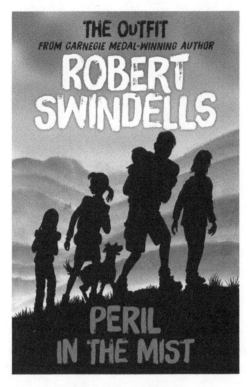

ISBN 978-1-78270-057-9

A challenging hike across five remote moors is just the sort of adventure The Outfit love. But when they find themselves alone on the moors as mist descends and night falls, will The Outfit be able to overcome their greatest challenge yet?

READ ALL OF THE OUTFIT'S THRILLING ADVENTURES!

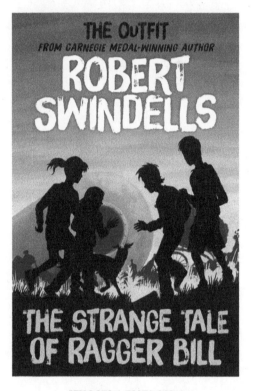

THE OUTFIT
FROM CARNEGIE MEDAL-WINNING AUTHOR
ROBERT SWINDELLS

THE STRANGE TALE OF RAGGER BILL

ISBN 978-1-78270-058-6

A little girl has gone missing and some
of the villagers are taking matters into their
own hands. Ragger Bill is the main suspect,
but The Outfit are sure he is innocent.
They must find the true culprit – and
fast – before things go too far!